Little Red Rosie

By Eric A. Kimmel

Illustrated by Mónica Gutierrez

A
Rosh Hashanah
Story

APPLES & HONEY PRESS

Springfield, NJ • Jerusalem

To Rachel, Wendy, and Marty
– EK

To my children, Sebastián and Simona,
who are still my babies
– MG

Apples & Honey Press
An imprint of Behrman House and Gefen Publishing House
Behrman House, 11 Edison Place, Springfield, New Jersey 07081
Gefen Publishing House Ltd., 6 Hatzvi Street, Jerusalem 94386, Israel
www.applesandhoneypress.com

ISBN 978-1-68115-518-0

Library of Congress Cataloging-in-Publication Data
Names: Kimmel, Eric A., author. | Gutierrez, Monica (Monica Graciela), 1960-
illustrator.
Title: Little Red Rosie : A Rosh Hashanah Story / by Eric A. Kimmel ; illustrated by Monica Gutierrez.
Description: Springfield, NJ : Apples & Honey Press, [2016] | Summary: In
this playful version of The Little Red Hen, a young girl enlists her bird
friends to help make the challah and host a house full of guests for Rosh
Hashanah.
Identifiers: LCCN 2015039496 | ISBN 9781681155180
Subjects: | CYAC: Jews--Folklore. | Rosh ha-Shanah--Fiction. | Challah
(Bread)--Fiction. | Bread--Fiction. | Baking--Fiction. | Birds--Fiction. |
Hospitality--Fiction. | Folklore.
Classification: LCC PZ8.1.K567 Li 2016 | DDC 296.4/315--dc23 LC record available at http://lccn.loc.gov/2015039496

Design by Alexandra Segal
Edited by Dena Neusner
Printed in Israel
9 8 7 6 5 4 3 2 1

Rosh Hashanah, the New Year, was on its way. Little Red Rosie promised to bake a loaf of challah bread for the neighborhood dinner.

"Time to get busy," Little Red Rosie said. "Who will help me measure the flour and make the dough?"

"I think I'd better do it myself,"

said Little Red Rosie.

"Who will help me knead the dough?" Little Red Rosie asked.

"I will," said Parrot.

"I will,"
said Hornbill.

"I will," said Toucan.

"Who will help me warm the dough so it can rise?" Little Red Rosie asked.

"I will," said Toucan.

"I will," said Parrot.

"I can do that," said Hornbill.

"Good job!" said Little Red Rosie.
"You sat on the dough like it
was an egg in a nest."

"Now who will help me shape
the dough into challah?"
Little Red Rosie asked.

"I will," said Toucan.

"I will," said Parrot.

"Let me!" said Hornbill.

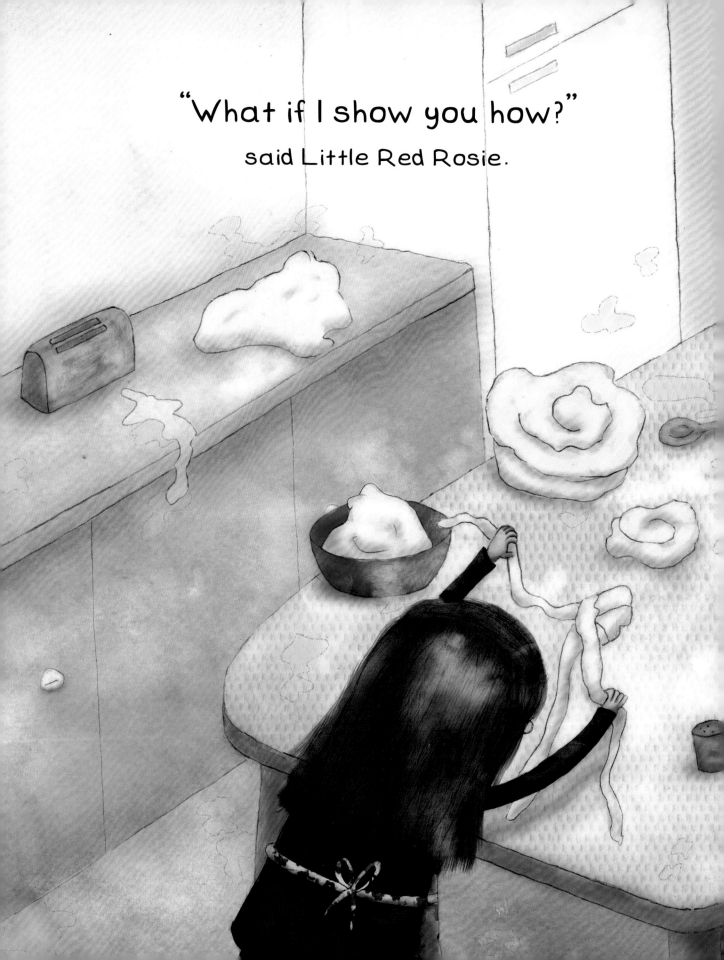

"What if I show you how?"
said Little Red Rosie.

"Now who will help me brush the challah with egg and sprinkle it with poppy seeds?" Little Red Rosie asked.

"I will," said Toucan.

"I will!" said Parrot.

"Oops!" said Hornbill.

"We can do this, yes we can,"

said Little Red Rosie.

"We're almost done,"

said Little Red Rosie.

"Who will help me clean the kitchen
while the challah bakes?"

"CAREFUL!
Don't drop that!"

"I think I'd better do this myself!"

said Little Red Rosie.

The challah baked to a golden brown. The neighbors began arriving. Little Red Rosie put the challah on the table with apples, honey, and other good things.

"Who will help me say the
blessing for the challah?"
Little Red Rosie asked.

"I will," said Toucan.

"I will," said Parrot.

"I know this by heart," said Hornbill.

"Let's hold hands and wings
as we say the words together,"
Little Red Rosie said.

"Praised are You,
Ruler of the world,
who brings forth
bread from the earth."

"Amen," said Toucan.
"Amen," said Parrot.
"Amen," said Hornbill.
"Good job!" said Rosie.

"Now who will help me
eat the challah?"
Little Red Rosie asked.

"I will," said Toucan.

"I will," said Parrot.

"WILL I!" said Hornbill.

"Of course you all will,"

said Little Red Rosie.

"I couldn't have done it without you."

Dear Friends,

Small children are often told not to interfere.
"You're too little. Leave that alone. You'll make a mess."
But children learn best by doing things themselves, even if they don't get it right at first. "Helping" often results in a mess! Children also learn through role-playing. Here, Rosie practices being the capable one—the parent—with her bird friends. She is learning the kindness, patience, and encouragement she will show to her own children when she grows up.

Rosh Hashanah is the perfect time for Rosie to practice becoming her best self. The holiday is a time to reflect on the past year and resolve to do our part to build a better world in the new year. In *Little Red Rosie*, the whole neighborhood joins in the Rosh Hashanah celebration. This emphasizes the universality at the heart of the holiday—we wish for a good year for everyone!

Welcoming guests (*hachnasat orchim* in Hebrew) is a mitzvah that goes back to the time of Abraham. A celebration is not complete unless we share it with others; especially those who may not have homes or families themselves.

What are some new ways you can reach out and be welcoming to others, on Rosh Hashanah and all year?

Shanah Tovah,

Eric